FOREWORD

Welcome Reader, to *Rhymecraft - Verses From Lancashire*.

Among these pages you will find a whole host of poetic gems, built from the ground up by some wonderful young minds. Included are a variety of poetic styles, from amazing acrostics to creative cinquains, from dazzling diamantes to fascinating free verse.

Here at Young Writers our objective has always been to help children discover the joys of poetry and creative writing. Few things are more encouraging for the aspiring writer than seeing their own work in print. We are proud that our anthologies are able to give young authors this unique sense of confidence and pride in their abilities as well as letting their poetry reach new audiences.

The editing process was a tough but rewarding one that allowed us to gain an insight into the blooming creativity of today's primary school pupils. I hope you find as much enjoyment and inspiration in the following poetry as I have, so much so that you pick up a pen and get writing!

Allie Jones

Verses From Lancashire

Edited By Allie Jones

First published in Great Britain in 2018 by:

Young Writers
Remus House
Coltsfoot Drive
Peterborough
PE2 9BF
Telephone: 01733 890066
Website: www.youngwriters.co.uk

CONTENTS

Fenn Alexander Burslam (9) 56
Rhys Sailsbury (9) 57
Sophie Marie Booth (10) 58
Zeke Braithwaite (9) 59
Clarkson Yao Yang Whittaker (9) 60

Lomeshaye Junior School, Nelson

Raabiah Imran (9) 61
Khadija Naseer (9) 62
Ayesha Adnan (10) 63

Our Lady Of Mount Carmel Catholic Primary School, Ashton-Under-Lyne

Eddie Liu (10) 64
Thomas Stackhouse (11) 65
Lucas Jones (10) 66
Jessica-Louise Spilsbury (10) 67
Nicole Juraszek (10) 68
Isabella Ablus Charles (10) 69
Chloe Calderbank (10) 70
Harry Redfearn (11) 71
Aimee Clegg (11) 72
Eloise May (10) 73
Alessio Cicchirillo-Bower (11) 74
Callum Wilson (10) 75
Caitlin Braun (10) 76
Martha Roberts (11) 77
Hamza Khan (10) 78
Abigail Mayers (10) 79

Queen's Drive Primary School, Fulwood

Katie Mann (9) 80
Sarah Leanne Buckler (9) 82
Amirah Vorajee (9) 84
Avneesh Desai (9) 86
Isabel Cole (9) 88
Sujit Reddy Velagala (9) 90
Lily Beatrice Cornall (9) 92
Hudhaifah Kazi (9) 94

Amnah Patel (9) 96
Asha Grace Al Alawi (9) 97
Dillon Bennison (9) 98
Mohammed Deen Saleh (9) 100
Saarah Patel (9) 101
Scott Bradley (9) 102
Hashim Ahmed Kazi (9) 103
Srainya Arakal (9) 104
Maisie-Belle Molloy (9) 105
Hibbah Maryam Patel (9) 106
Aafiyah Patel (9) 108
Arya Jayakrishnan (9) 109
Ibrahim Moosa (9) 110
Anand Singh (10) 111
Adam Member (9) & Aimee Jade Tilley 112
Megan Casey (10) 113
Eesaa Member (9) 114
Poppy Billington (9) 115
Medhansh Nandwana (9) 116
Blake Hallas (10) 117
Omar Abdou (9) 118
Eva Dawson (9) 119
Chloe Donnelly (9) 120
Thomas Hutton (9) 121
Aamena Patel (9) 122
Jaxon (9) 123
Aidan Lee (9) 124
Mariyah Musa (9) 125
Lucie Smith (9) 126
Amber Hussain (9) 127
Zara Mann (9) 128
Anoosha Khan (10) 129
Amirah Patel (9) 130
Amirah Adnan Ahmed (9) 131
Ebony Julianne Cerqua (10) 132
Zakaria Ahmed (10) 133
Anna Bradford (9) 134
Muhammad Randeri (9) 135
Andrew Richard Hugh Donaldson (9) 136
Ibraheem Aziz (9) 137

St Agnes CE Primary School, Lees

Daisy Gittins (7)	138
Logan Allison (8)	139
Joshua White (9)	140
Isabella Josephine Holcroft (7)	141
Scarlett Summer Lees (8)	142
Ethan Smith (10)	143
William Thomas Sever (7)	144
Emily Grace Bertram (7)	145
Ava Grace McNally (8)	146

St Bartholomew's CE Primary School, Great Harwood

Oliver Tucker (9)	147
Jessica Catherine Rowe (8)	148
Connor Lewis Woods (8)	149
Tara McIntosh (9)	150
Katie Balderson (10)	151
Joshua Duckworth (9)	152

St John With St Michael CE Primary School, Shawforth

Chloe Chaffer (9)	153
Charlie Careswell (8)	154
Cameron Rae Blackburn-Smith (7)	155
Caitlin Taylor (7)	156
Natalie Varnom (7)	157
Bailey Fletcher (8)	158
Imogen Steel (7)	159
Natasha Holmes (7)	160
Libby Duff (9)	161

THE POEMS

My Life

When I'm one I crawl down the hall,
I crawl upstairs and fall on my bum!
When I don't get food I scream and bawl,
You can hear me down the hall.
When I'm two I start to talk and walk,
I don't want to get up.
Anyhow, I eat a lot.
When someone fights me I fight back.
I whinge as well.
When I'm three I start going to nursery
But I poo and wee.
I also punch and eat lunch
And fight and bite, I hate termites.
When I'm 25 I'm going to be on X Factor
And be in the semi-finals.
I'm going to impress Simon Cowell.

Damien Flintoft (8)
Blackpool Gateway Academy, Blackpool

Crazy Football

The players walked onto the pitch.
The refs followed them out.
The captains walked onto the pitch.
There were loads of fans about.

The whole team walked onto the pitch.
On the pitch there was a high ditch.
The defender kicked the ball,
The striker kicked the ball and it hit the wall.

The fans started to throw bottles
And the players started to throw waffles.
The player started to argue.
The fans started to moo.

The ref blew the whistle for the end of the match.
The ref blows off his watch.

Sam Brown (8)
Blackpool Gateway Academy, Blackpool

Minecraft

The sheep grow like my school top.
The zombies are green like the dirty grass
And the pigs are pink like Miss Hind's eyes.
The cows are coloured like brown poo
And the white colour's like a piece of paper
And the red apples are a like a red bullseye.
The water is blue like in the sky.
The chickens are white like a cloud.
The bow of a skeleton is wooden like a tree.
The coal is black like a shark's eyes.
The cute cheetah is yellow like a bright sun.
The horse is as cute as a teddy bear.
The grass is as shiny as a metal robot.

Jamie Lee (8)
Blackpool Gateway Academy, Blackpool

Nutter Football

We are travelling to London.
We are very excited.
The coach is taking a very long time.

We finally get there,
Our mums have finally arrived.
We get out of the coach,
Our mums have survived.

All the players go to the changing room.
Our kit's colour is red and brown.
Time is ticking, I have to zoom.
Time is getting closer.

We start to wait on the stairs.
We all shake the players' hands.
I have beautiful fans.
They are all cheering my name.
I will be on the Wall of Fame.

Dylan Alwyn Jerome (9)
Blackpool Gateway Academy, Blackpool

The Queen Of Winter

I wish I was a queen,
I would be dressed in emerald-green.

When you become king,
We will sing a song in the grass, we will in the wind.

I will live in a castle with my dog, Basil,
He will have to listen when I whistle.
Soon he will be grown up.
After that he won't be a pup.

I'd love to have a pink bedroom,
Maybe with a wink it might appear.

I look at my hair, I stop and stare,
My hair has a large bow in the low bit.

Aliyah Ahmed (8)
Blackpool Gateway Academy, Blackpool

Minecraft Mod Craft!

I'm in a new world,
The world is as bumpy as a rock.
I went to a dark, spooky cave with lots of rocks.
I found a castle, it was new, now it is old.
The dark, old castle was very cold.
I went back to the creepy cave,
I found a creepy house with a bed.
I found a very creepy creeper.
He blew up.
I started to build my house.
I think I placed a million blocks.
I saw diamond ore.

Ubaid Khan (9)
Blackpool Gateway Academy, Blackpool

Unicorn Dreams

My unicorn's fur is as bright as snow
And its hair is as bright as the pink in the sunset.
Its eyes are sparkly brown.
When it runs on the grass its pink, sparkly tail
Blows like a bird's wings,
Its mane blows in the wind like a beautiful
sparrow.
My unicorn and I fly through the trees,
I feel magic,
When I'm with my friends I feel safe.

Maddy Ashworth (8)
Blackpool Gateway Academy, Blackpool

Three Pigs And The Farmer

The farmer fed his pigs with milk
And the villagers made some silk.

The farmer let the chickens go
And the electricity was low.

The pigs ate all the food
And the neighbours were very rude.

The farmer ate one pig
And I had to dig.

I made a grave for Pinky,
I feel very inky.

Oskar Nowak (8)
Blackpool Gateway Academy, Blackpool

Magical Unicorns

Unicorns, unicorns, unicorns,
They are harmless and magic,
But do you want to know a secret?
All unicorns are magical and soft.
They have lots of power to the world
And are all nice
Except the mean ones,
They are horrible and mean,
They think they have power,
Anyway I love unicorns, unicorns, unicorns.

Scarlett Shanice Walker (8)

Blackpool Gateway Academy, Blackpool

How A Dog And A Cat Are Different

My dog breathes air and my cat has hair.
My cat was bold, now he's old.
My dog called Groovy ate the gravy.
My cat called Dotty was very spotty.
My dog slips down the hall and bumps the wall.
My dog was cold now he's old.
My cat saw a bear and the dog got scared.
My dog was scared but my cat never cared.

Alisha Hannaford (8)

Blackpool Gateway Academy, Blackpool

Minecraft, Minecraft

I've got to turn on the PC.
Turn on the video so they can see, see.
Minecraft is coming today.
I'm making a new video every day.
Using zombies like slaves.
I've got a diamond mansion bro.
I'm using iron like a pro.
You got to keep the flow.
Only gods can come in my house, yo.

Jaden Lightbourne (8)
Blackpool Gateway Academy, Blackpool

The Holidays

(Inspired by the 'The Magic Box' by Kit Wright)

I put in the box...
Some old, good and dusty memories,
A lovely and flowery bucket full of some wrinkly shells,
Some colourful sunglasses shining out of the box,
Some pictures of the beautiful, noisy and tidy hotel,
A huge notebook full of plans and adventures,
A camera full of pictures and memories.

Nicola Bak (8)
Blackpool Gateway Academy, Blackpool

Untitled

My mum and dad are in the house.
We're going to the forest to go to the camp,
On for the hunt for a little red fish.
We're in the car to go to the woods with our red car.
We're in the woods in the beautiful nature.
We're in the woods, we're making a camp
And now it's done.

Blazej Brandon Szczecinski (8)
Blackpool Gateway Academy, Blackpool

School

School is back,
School is here,
School is fun
And we're back for a brand-new year.
Here we come, here we go,
So let's start learning till the end
But if you don't I will make you squirm
So listen up or you will go down a grade,
So be good all the time which is best of all.

Destiny Ramshaw (8)

Blackpool Gateway Academy, Blackpool

My Favourite Holiday

(Inspired by the 'The Magic Box' by Kit Wright)

I will put in the box...
The cold, wet, wobbly sea,
The yellow silky sand tickling my toes,
The dazzling seashells like a white pebble.

In my box I will put...
Slimy green, swishing seaweed,
The hairy, fresh, brown, big coconuts,
The hot, shiny, boiling sun.

Harley Ball (7)
Blackpool Gateway Academy, Blackpool

Roblox

Roblox is here
And you can play here.
A beautiful place
Where you can play.
Different aims
With different names.
Roblox is a good game,
I mean a good game.
Do you think it's a good game
Or what about an aim?
I like Roblox
Or should I say goblox?

McKenzie Bayliss (8)
Blackpool Gateway Academy, Blackpool

Salina Green

Salina,
Kind, funny and nice,
Brother of Tom, Blake and Callum,
Lover of painting, drawing and colouring,
Who feels happy and full of life,
Who gives happiness and laughter,
Who fears spiders and water,
Who wears pretty clothes,
Who lives in Blackpool,
Green.

Salina Green (8)
Blackpool Gateway Academy, Blackpool

The Legend Sword

As two
warriors
meet their
fate again,
swords
clash so
hard it
hurts my
ears. You use
it by
gripping
the hands and swinging your arm
to attack, block your face to defend
yourself. The Legend Sword
made of really
strong iron.

Charlie Gallagher (8)
Blackpool Gateway Academy, Blackpool

Roller Coaster

R is for roller coaster so speedy and bright
O is for over the loop-the-loop
L is for laughter all the way down
L is for loop-the-loop
E is for everyone screaming and crying
R is for riding a carriage.

Alice Cooper (7)

Blackpool Gateway Academy, Blackpool

Minecraft

M is for mining

I is for interactive

N is for Nether

E is for eggs

C is for creative

R is for riding

A is for awesome

F is for flint and steel

T is for teleport.

James Radford (7)

Blackpool Gateway Academy, Blackpool

Minecraft Universe

Bom and Tom went to Earth.
They saw Minecraft zombies.
Bom and Tom went to Jupiter.
The creepers are Endies.
Bom and Tom went to the moon.
It was dark and scary.
Bom and Tom went to the sun.
It was hot and blurry.

Oliver Smith (8)
Blackpool Gateway Academy, Blackpool

Back To School

Summer is over and fall is here,
Back to school for a brand new year,
Sit down and cross your feet,
Hands in your lap, nice and neat.
Be sure you learn
Or the teacher will make you squirm.
Now we are ready to start our day.

Aidan Williamson (8)
Blackpool Gateway Academy, Blackpool

Dreams

Not plain but cute,
Can make a sound of a flute.
Sparkly but not frightening,
Beautifully pink,
Has a trick
To make the boys wink.
Has a purple mane
That blows in the wind.
Beautiful like a princess.

Jenna Leigh Wright (8)
Blackpool Gateway Academy, Blackpool

Aeroplane Zoom

There it goes down the runway,
Ripping up the tarmac.
It's a massive bird in the sky.
From Earth it looks like a tiny bird.
Aeroplanes fly across the world,
Zooming through the clouds.

James Crampton (8)

Blackpool Gateway Academy, Blackpool

The Magic Box

(Inspired by 'The Magic Box' by Kit Wright)

I will put in my box...
The yummy smell from chocolate,
The swish of lots of lions' tails,
Lovely sounds of birds' wings.

I will put in my box...
The chewy taste of marshmallows,
The princess and knights dancing in the moonlight.

I will put in my box...
Three wizards casting a spell,
An ice cube that fell in a well.

My box is fashioned from...
A unicorn's magic,
A galaxy with fireworks,
Gold, rubies and a daisy crown.

Niamh Erin Williams (7)

Claypool Primary School, Horwich

The Magic Of The World

(Inspired by 'The Magic Box' by Kit Wright)

A little bit of soft sand from a white beach,
Crystals as cold as ice,
A cold swish of rapid wind.
A couple of butterflies, they are flies but beautiful,
Some white clouds out of the blue sky,
Sparkles of a gold dress,
A black sheep's wool as soft as a dog's fur
That is so cuddly.

My box is fashioned from the soft, silky cover of a
blanket,
In the corners there are whispers of friendly voices,
All on the lid, soft like a cushion in colours
Of red and white.

Angel Jones (7)
Claypool Primary School, Horwich

Seasons

In spring we all have a sing,
We all have a sing in a ring.
The flowers pop out and have a quick hop.
We all lead the way and stay at the top.

In autumn the leaves fall on the ground
Dancing like a bird.
All the birds are singing a lovely song
Whilst having a curl.

In winter I get comfy in bed,
The days are getting quicker and it's bitter.
I sit in winter
And I'm cold, it looks like I'm a sitter.

In summer it's so hot
And we stretch our legs but our legs get hot.
I'm so squashed because there's a bunch of people
And more; there's a lot.

Khadijah Islam (7)
Gaskell Community Primary School, Bolton

A Wet Day

I had a party but it was wet.
It was really wet but not getting dried yet.
There was a puddle,
My mum gave a cuddle.
I saw a cat wearing a wet hat
Give a cuddle but not a quick cuddle.
No more ice cream.
I saw someone eating cream.
I bought some sweets but I'm not sweet.
I saw a cat but not a bat,
I saw a rainbow but not a tawny owl.
I just yawned but it's not just dawn.

I ate an amazing thing in the rain,
A splashing thing.
I don't know what to say,
This is an amazing day!

Alishba Zafar (7)
Gaskell Community Primary School, Bolton

Fantastic Friendship

Friendship can be about love
Or it can be about worry.
You might tell an adult.
If you have worries don't keep it in.
I am going to tell you a little rhyme.

Any kind of worry, any bit of bother
Have a funny tummy,
So don't let your bother get bigger,
So don't be afraid to tell and share.

Friendship is cool just like school.
Friendship is good and sometimes it is a fool.
It makes me laugh and makes me cry
And makes me and my friends cry.

Ameerah Kiani (8)
Gaskell Community Primary School, Bolton

Seasons

I like it when it is summer
Because we can go to the beach
And go to the park.
Then we get six weeks holiday
And wear shorts and have ice cream.

Spring: I like it because newborn chicks come alive,
So do pigs as well.

Winter: It is Christmas and we get snow
And get to have a snowball fight
And build a snowman and wear your cold clothes.

Autumn: The leaves change colour
And the leaves come off the trees
And it is cold.

Ibrahim Iqbal (8)
Gaskell Community Primary School, Bolton

Horrid Henry

I know a boy named Horrid Henry,
For his pocket money is just one penny
And his brother, Perfect Peter, gets lots every day,
But Mum still has to pay.
Henry wants Peter to pay,
If he does Henry will give him pocket money every
day.
Henry's dad has a shiny car,
It can go very far.
Right now Henry's a dinosaur
But Peter's leg is still very sore.
Henry has a hamster called Fang,
I also have two fangs.

Zain Malik (7)
Gaskell Community Primary School, Bolton

Good Friendship

Friendship is a test for whoever is the best.
My friend who once fell,
I could tell she was going to yell.
My best friend was reading me a book
And she let me have a look.
My friend, Ameerah, who has really got the trend
Is cool because she is my friend.

My friend is cool just like school.
Me and my friend are fantastic
Because we do gymnastic.
I once thought I was a fool
But then they all called me cool.

Falak Khawaja (8)
Gaskell Community Primary School, Bolton

Untitled

Warm,
Go to the seaside,
Go to a friend's house,
Go to the beach,
Go to the park,
Go to the funfair,
Go to the aeroplane,
Go to the countryside,
Go to the jungle,
Go to watch movies,
Go to cousins,
Go to play on the park,
Go to a wedding,
Go to school,
Go to new houses,
Go to play with your dolls,
Play in summer,
Play with sandcastles,
Go find new friends!

Lauren Mathkur (7)
Gaskell Community Primary School, Bolton

Friendship

I have friends who could play PS4
Who come and play the PS3.
I like my friends,
They like me.

I have a pen
And have a hen.

I am afraid of ghosts
But I have so many friends.

I have cereals
That are called Weetabix.

I don't like watching horror movies that are scary.
A rainbow sitting in the sky like a plane can fly.

Jaffar Faraz (8)
Gaskell Community Primary School, Bolton

I Love Cats And Dogs

I love dogs, you should too,
I love cats and so do you.
I have cats, I like bats,
I like cats more than bats.
I love dogs because they're cute,
I like cats like a bag of loot.
Do you like cats?
I like them too.
I am drinking a cup of juice.
Some dogs don't, some dogs do,
They better not bite you.
If you bite one, they'll bite you
And they will chase you.

Logan Dean Baker (7)
Gaskell Community Primary School, Bolton

Winter

Winter is the best season!
You get to wear lots of snuggly clothes.
So look in this book to see what winter is all about!
When the snow falls delicately make
Snow angels in the snow,
Make snowmen, put a hat and a scarf
And a carrot for its nose.
Make big footprints!
Hide treasure for somebody to seek and find!
It's a blanket of snow!
It's like one million snowflakes!

Juwairiyah Patel (7)
Gaskell Community Primary School, Bolton

Awesome Dreams

Dreams scare so be aware
And don't look up at your dreams that scare.
Your dreams come true
But sometimes they might not come true.
Dreams are cool just like school!
I love my dreams and I love my science team.
What if you had a dream about somebody mean?
Dreams are there, happy to be bare.
Be aware, because dreams are there!

Fatima Hameeda (7)
Gaskell Community Primary School, Bolton

Imaginations

Imagination is fun,
It's like you're in the sun.
They make you dream
About something wonderful you've never seen.
Imagination is like dreams, so beautiful to see.
Maybe you'll explore something more,
So imagination makes you dream
You're invited to a celebration,
Enjoying the sun,
You're having fun.

Abdullah Ahmed (7)
Gaskell Community Primary School, Bolton

Minecraft

Minecraft is fun because you can craft.
The skies are smooth and the water is cool.
You can climb, you can be put in slime.
Why can you die? But you can fly.
How do you get pets? You can have pots.
I can fly, I can be sly.
You can sit, you can pick.
You can see, you can drink and eat.
We can skip.
We can swim.

Hamza Altaf Patel (7)
Gaskell Community Primary School, Bolton

Jets

I love jets,
they make me jump in nets.
They shoot bullets to the ground,
to make people frown.
They're staring at the shutters,
to aim at gutters.
It is fast,
so it can go past.
They don't go in the mud
because their engine will not be good.
I am looking for jets
because I am right in my net.

Raza Ahmed (7)
Gaskell Community Primary School, Bolton

Dreams

When I have dreams
I feel like I am an ice cream!

I taste like a candy,
I look like a wild dandy.

When I have a bad dream
I really look like a gleam.

I dream in my sleep
When my legs kick and leap.

Dreams are soft as candyfloss!

Saman Irshad (7)
Gaskell Community Primary School, Bolton

Untitled

My sisters are sunshine
And my sisters are rain!
My sisters are thunder and lightning
And back to sunshine again!
My sisters are the sunshine
When they're kind to me
And when they're rain they like to be nosy
And when they are thunder and lightning
They're angry!

Annie McQuaide (7)

Gaskell Community Primary School, Bolton

Untitled

He is ugly like a monster,
He is like a horrid boy that's crazy!
He is so mean like a wild animal in the house.
He is like Where's Wally?
He is very mean, he is crazy and lazy.
He is not funny.
He doesn't like to share secrets.
He is really scary like a zombie.

Maria Csonka (7)
Gaskell Community Primary School, Bolton

Untitled

Nice summer, beautiful summer,
Calm, lovely, peaceful beach!
You can eat ice lollies all day long,
Cold as an iceberg.
My tongue is as white as a sheep.
The ice is really, really cold
And the beach is as lovely as a bright light sun.
You can eat your ice lolly.

Katie Rayment (8)
Gaskell Community Primary School, Bolton

Untitled

Happy, scary,
Evil green peas
Waiting for me,
To get me and eat me
But I am too late,
It is coming to get me
And I am not happy
Because it is coming very fast.
My mum is coming and she said it is dinner time
But I am too scared!

Adiba Sahar (7)
Gaskell Community Primary School, Bolton

Zeus Was A Dude!

Zeus was a dude, Zeus was a dude in 90BC.
Zeus was a dude, Zeus was a dude in 80BC,
In 90BC, in 80BC, Zeus was a dude,
Zeus was a dude in 70BC,
In 90BC, in 80BC, in 70BC, Zeus was a dude,
Zeus was a dude in 60BC,
In 90BC, in 80BC, in 70BC, in 60BC, Zeus was a dude.
Zeus was a dude in 50BC,
In 90BC, in 80BC, in 70BC, in 60BC, in 50BC, Zeus was a dude.
Zeus was a dude in 40BC,
In 90BC, in 80BC, in 70BC, in 60BC, in 50BC.
In 40BC, Zeus was a dude,
Zeus was a dude in 30BC,
In 90BC, in 80BC, in 70BC, in 60BC, in 50BC, in 40BC, in 30BC, Zeus was a dude.
Zeus was a dude in 20BC.
In 90BC, in 80BC, in 70BC, in 60BC, in 50BC,
In 40BC, in 30BC, in 20BC. Zeus was a dude,

Zeus was a dude in 10BC,
In 90BC, in 80BC, in 70BC, in 60BC, in 50BC,
In 40BC, in 30BC, in 20BC, in 10BC,
Zeus was a dude!

Millie Jones (10)
Lancaster Lane Community Primary School, Clayton-Le-Woods

The Trojan Horse

The leader jumps out the Trojan horse,
Goes forward, knocks on the door,
He slips back in the horse again
And tells his plan to all.
'Shush, don't holler, quiet down.
They're coming at you, you can hear them now.
Listen to them talking praise,
They don't know we're in here,' he says.
'What a pretty horse,' they natter,
'Let's take it and show the master.'
'They've fallen for it,' the warriors whisper.
'In 3, 2, 1, jump out and kill them.'
They all jump out!
The people shout!
'We all are going to die!'
And right they were
Because that day
Many people in dismay
Got sliced and quartered, come what may
Did some people live? Who knows?

Efini Morgan (10)

Lancaster Lane Community Primary School, Clayton-Le-Woods

Hades' Revenge

Once Hades went to Zeus
To get his golden goose.

Zeus said, 'No
You big foe
Let's have a fight
To see who has the right
To have the golden goose.'

Zeus swung his lightning bolt
While Hades was about to unfold.

Hades went with a zap
Right on his six-pack
And Hades struck to the ground.
Hades crawled to the golden goose
And then Zeus felt like a moose.
Then Hades disappeared in a poof
Just so Zeus had no proof.

Daniel Patterson (9)
Lancaster Lane Community Primary School, Clayton-Le-Woods

Poseidon, God Of The Sea

Poseidon is the god of the sea,
He's got a lot of powers as you can see,
He makes waves as big as a tower,
He also makes it rain and shower.
The seas are bright and blue,
Also like his light blue shoes.
Zeus' brother he was, and was very old as I was told.
Poseidon is also the god of storms and earthquakes,
I've told you about Poseidon and given you the key,
I hope you understand that Poseidon is the god of the sea.

Lucy Chapman (9)

Lancaster Lane Community Primary School, Clayton-Le-Woods

Untitled

Once there was a big, greedy god
That kept on eating people and animals.
He had a big round tummy
The looked all gummy.
He couldn't fit in his bed,
He had a pet that sat on his head,
Because he fell
And went in the cell.
This god is called Hades,
He has a wife called Madies.
All Madies does is eat ladies.
They were that greedy they ate a house
And saw a mouse in the house.

Grace Olivia Jean Loughlin (9)

Lancaster Lane Community Primary School, Clayton-Le-Woods

Saving Aphrodite

Once there was a houralish
That found a human fish
Lying at the bottom of the sea
And it went wild and free.
It brought her up to the land
With the hot sand,
It was burning hot sand,
The burning hot sand gave her a hand,
It warmed her up
While she read a book.
She got magical powers,
Then she built towers.
The houralish is made with
A horse, whale and a fish.

Isabelle Ainsley (9)
Lancaster Lane Community Primary School, Clayton-Le-Woods

Alexander The Great

Alexander the Great,
Well he wasn't so great
But let's just go with it.
He sent some men
To conquer the world, he wanted all of it.
While his troops went to take over,
Alexander the Great told the chief, Ava,
To go to the centre of the Earth,
To slice it in half.
We will do some others like Mars.
And this is why he is not so great
Because he is in a grave.

Alex Gray (10)
Lancaster Lane Community Primary School, Clayton-Le-Woods

Rabphin And The Carrfish Leaves (Rabbits Eat Carrots And Dolphins Eat Fish)

Rabphin is my creature
The one and only
He has lots of features
Holding each and every one.

He goes for a swim in the deep blue sea
To find a tunnel
Full of carrfish leaves
He finds hidden treasure
To find his face in pleasure.

He gobbles them all up
All very happy
But now he has no more
He is very snappy.

Olivia Gatley (10)

Lancaster Lane Community Primary School, Clayton-Le-Woods

The Minotaur

The Minotaur's roar was horrifically loud,
As loud as a nuclear bomb...
It reached the gods high up in the clouds,
It was fiercely long.

Theseus came, to beat the Minotaur's game,
But then the Minotaur roared again
And then Theseus pulled and whipped out his sword
And hacked off the Minotaur's head.

Zak Whittaker (9)

Lancaster Lane Community Primary School, Clayton-Le-Woods

Hades' Excuse To Zeus

One day Hades was hanging around
In his scary castle under the ground.
Then he got bored and got in his chariot,
Then he found a maiden called Harriet.
They went up to Mount Olympus
And Harriet felt a bit delirious.
They went to Zeus and had an excuse
To steal his lightning bolts,
then Zeus turned and started a revolt.

Fenn Alexander Burslam (9)

Lancaster Lane Community Primary School, Clayton-Le-Woods

Ares' Life Story

There once was a god called Ares
Who was big, bad and scary.
He loved to start wars
With his monstrous claws
Until he met a girl called Mary.

So now he's perfectly nice,
He is sweeter than sugar and spice.
Mary is always getting flowers
That she looks at for hours
And now he is cooler than ice.

Rhys Sailsbury (9)

Lancaster Lane Community Primary School, Clayton-Le-Woods

A Wolf Poem

The sun was shining through the trees
As the creature awoke.
When the creature awoke
He sensed danger.
He went to the jungle city
To see what was going on.
It was a robbery
But the robber got away
And then it was over.

Sophie Marie Booth (10)

Lancaster Lane Community Primary School, Clayton-Le-Woods

Poseidon

There once was a god called Poseidon
Who ruled the ocean blue,
A seahorse chariot to ride on,
Over every inch he knew.

He's Zeus' brother,
His trident's rubber,
He's wetter
Than a flooded house.

Zeke Braithwaite (9)

Lancaster Lane Community Primary School, Clayton-Le-Woods

The Hydra
(A diamante poem)

Hydra
Deadly, gigantic
Scaly, stomping, chomping
Ruling, burning, killing, destroying
Unstoppable, spikes, embers
Crushing, splitting
Hypnotising.

Clarkson Yao Yang Whittaker (9)
Lancaster Lane Community Primary School, Clayton-Le-Woods

Cute Cats Don't Care

Cats don't care what dogs think,
They just look down and sort of wink.
Perch themselves way up high,
The dogs bark and start to cry.
it's really not fair, those agile cats
Hiding in places just like rats.
The dogs want to play, join in the fun,
Chase that cat, make it run.
But cats care less, don't need to play fair,
Like to chase, don't have a care.
Poor dog sits and wonders why?
Sly old cat naps within sight.
Dogs keep guard, watching for a twitch.
Cats don't move, not even an inch.
The game goes on, cats unaware,
Dogs just plead, please care.

Raabiah Imran (9)
Lomeshaye Junior School, Nelson

Dreams, Oh Dreams

I am glad to be me,
That is because I follow my amazing dreams.
I take the right zone
But I am careful I don't trip on a stone.
Right now my dreams are floating in a bubble to
Dreamland because that's where they come true.

Lightning is running through the sky,
Just like my dreams are drawing pictures of me,
Then I just think there is no one else to see.

Dreams, oh dreams, I am glad to be
That is because I follow my dreams.
I take the right zone
But I am careful I don't trip on a stone.

Dreams here I come.

Khadija Naseer (9)
Lomeshaye Junior School, Nelson

Mixed Emotions

M any of us feel
I nquisitive
X enophobic
E xcited
D epressed

E nthusiastic
M iserable
O verjoyed
T errific
I nterested
O dd
N eglected
S hy

At times we all feel the same
Even though we don't all have an identical name.

Ayesha Adnan (10)

Lomeshaye Junior School, Nelson

What Nature Really Is

Look, listen... into the jungle I go.
What can I hear? What can I see?
Look at the trees and vines, how tall they grow!
Many green shades; coloured are the leaves on the tree.

Hear the vines rattle through the blazing breeze.
Listen, the monkeys jump from tree to tree.
Let the water flow, look at all the bees.
Swish! Swoosh! Look at the monkeys swinging free.

A river of colour crosses my feet,
I dare not move, I stand still as can be.
A cobra! A danger! You never want to meet,
If I don't move, it won't see me.

I push through the jungle, a wall of heat
Blasts my body, makes my head spin.
I'm sticky and thirsty, I feel deadbeat,
The jungle is deadly, nature will win.

Eddie Liu (10)
Our Lady Of Mount Carmel Catholic Primary School, Ashton-Under-Lyne

Ocean Life (An Acrostic Poem)

U nder the sea there is nothing to do

N othing to see but the colour blue

D estruction is here, more commonly known

E veryone says it's pollution, it's called that at home

R ewards are shallow, just like the tide

W hilst up there, kids filled with pride

A re digging up sand and placing junk in the sea

T his is killing off fish and it's bothering me

E ven though scientists are trying to help

R eally they are just making us yelp.

L ife under the ocean is rough

I am fed up and this is enough

F ish hate the ocean life, that is absurd

E ven breathing cannot be heard.

Thomas Stackhouse (11)

Our Lady Of Mount Carmel Catholic Primary School, Ashton-Under-Lyne

The Top, Pop, Hip Hop Rhyme

So I'm here to talk about music,
Let's start by talking about grime,
Dizzie Rascal, Stormzy and Skepta,
They all make their lyrics rhyme.

Next, let's go to the charts,
To talk about music called pop,
You can like it from age 0 to 100
And like the Beastie Boys 'Let the Beat Drop'.

On a plane let's go to Ibiza,
Where DJs play tunes to make you dance,
In a loud nightclub with flashing lights,
Let's listen to techno, rave and trance.

Lastly pick up your guitar
And let's strum it to make some rock.
Just like Bill Haley and His Comets,
'We're Gonna Rock Around the Clock'.

Lucas Jones (10)
Our Lady Of Mount Carmel Catholic Primary School, Ashton-Under-Lyne

The Night

All is quiet and still,
Darkness descends.
A hoot in the distance.
A lone bark of a wolf, looking for its mate.
The moon appears from behind a cloud
Lighting the Earth below.
The howls of the pack echo around
Until the moon disappears again.
The flash of a white tail, bobbing about,
Shows where a hare is darting about.
Suddenly there's a rustling noise.
As an owl swoops down and picks up its prey.
Then the moon disappears again.
Little lights shine in the black of night
As fireflies swoop and dart about.
The first rays of sun begin to appear
Lighting the sky,
As we say goodbye to the night
And hello to the day.

Jessica-Louise Spilsbury (10)

Our Lady Of Mount Carmel Catholic Primary School, Ashton-Under-Lyne

I Like April

I like April,
It's very warm in April,
That's the time when it's my birthday
And my brother's too!

In April I get to play outside more,
On the first of April, it's April Fool's Day,
Sometimes I can't think of what pranks to do
And my brother always guesses and finds out!

In April loads of new sets of flowers grow,
Some are purple, some are blue,
Some are pink and yellow too,
Every morning the birds sing
And sometimes I wish to be a bird!

I really like April,
The beautiful animals come out to play,
Squirrels, bunnies, birds, bees
And trees grow too!

Nicole Juraszek (10)

Our Lady Of Mount Carmel Catholic Primary School, Ashton-Under-Lyne

The Life Of Minecraft

My skin has black hair, ripped jeans
And a flower headband,
Just to show what I like.
In the dark there are monsters trying to get me.
I have nothing to fear because
I can lure them into an attack,
But I gotta watch my back!
Cats are good for scaring the creepers away
And a dog is a good teammate in a battle.
The one thing that me
And my dog teammate hate most is the end
Because a dagger lurks in the dark waiting for you.
There is no moon but it's always night.
He was born with great powers so beware,
His blood runs icy cold.

Isabella Ablus Charles (10)
Our Lady Of Mount Carmel Catholic Primary School, Ashton-
Under-Lyne

How Beautiful Are The Sun And Stars?

How beautiful are the sun and stars?
Let the sun say hi and the stars say hiya,
The sun was on fire!
Could it get any higher?
As the sun set and the stars rose up,
The stars twinkled as I wrinkled,
How beautiful are the sun and stars?

How beautiful are the sun and stars?
Let the sun say hi and the stars say bye,
The sun was huge!
Who would you choose, the sun or the stars?
As the sun set and stars rose up,
the stars brightened and I lightened,
How beautiful are the sun and stars?

Chloe Calderbank (10)

Our Lady Of Mount Carmel Catholic Primary School, Ashton-Under-Lyne

My Life

My life is football, my life is sport,
Everywhere I go I want to do more.
Even on the beach,
Even on the shore,
Volleyball, beachball and swimming,
They're all sports.
Where there is water, I am playing them for sure.
How do I feel while playing football, basketball
Or cricket?
Passion, excitement and elation.
All of these are what I feel every time
I step out onto the field.
They will all help me throughout my life
So when I feel down I'll turn that frown upside
down.

Harry Redfearn (11)
Our Lady Of Mount Carmel Catholic Primary School, Ashton-
Under-Lyne

Animals, Animals, Animals!

Lots come from eggs,
Most come with fins and even sometimes,
They have four legs!
Some cheep!
Some clutter!
Maybe they can fly
Or maybe they can creep!
Some that will slither
And some that will run.
Some come with feathers
Or maybe even none!
Animals' eggs are small
Or just as big as a bouncy ball.
The animals mentioned
Are quite a few.
They can hatch from eggs
Or lay them too!

Aimee Clegg (11)

Our Lady Of Mount Carmel Catholic Primary School, Ashton-Under-Lyne

World War One

W orld in danger
O ur lives depend on the soldiers
R evolting trenches
L ice crawling everywhere
D one, I wish it was done

W ar
A ll these lives wasted
R emember these boys and men

O ne last time families wish they could see their hero
N ever-ending
E very night bombs.

Eloise May (10)

Our Lady Of Mount Carmel Catholic Primary School, Ashton-Under-Lyne

The Cat And The Mouse

The cat ran through the house,
Trying to get the mouse.
The mouse climbed up the clock setting off the
bell,
As the cat ran, he tripped and fell.
The mouse laughed and thought, *this is a dream!*
The mouse jumped over the cat
And landed in a hat.
The cat looked with hunger in his eyes
And thought, *I can make some mouse pies!*

Alessio Cicchirillo-Bower (11)

Our Lady Of Mount Carmel Catholic Primary School, Ashton-
Under-Lyne

Bullying

Bullying is bad cos it makes people sad,
It can make our parents and teachers mad!

Do not be a fool, keep it cool,
Have some respect, we're not all perfect.

Love one another as God would want.
Let's play nice or ask for advice.

There's lots of support, do not suffer,
Just speak out and love each other.

Callum Wilson (10)
Our Lady Of Mount Carmel Catholic Primary School, Ashton-Under-Lyne

Halloween Night

Halloween night, won't you get a fright,
The big moon glowing
And the cold north wind blowing.
Rat-a-tat-tat at the door,
I grab some sweets from the floor.
As they sing trick or treat
I say, 'Would you like a sweet?'
Oh to see the joy on the street,
Halloween night, trick or treat.

Caitlin Braun (10)

Our Lady Of Mount Carmel Catholic Primary School, Ashton-Under-Lyne

Welcome To The Night

(Inspired by 'Welcome to the Night' by Joyce Sidman)

To all of you who scramble and peep,
Who buzz and hoot and crawl and creep.
Who wake without sun from their daytime sleep,
Welcome to the night!

To you who make the forest sing,
Who run and jump on foot and wing,
Who flutter, hover, bang and spring,
Welcome to the night!

Martha Roberts (11)
Our Lady Of Mount Carmel Catholic Primary School, Ashton-Under-Lyne

About Winter

W inter, it's basically a wonderland
　I ce is very thin and slippery
　N othing is hot, so all is cold
　T he weather is jaw-shaking
　E verything you touch makes you shiver
　R eally, extremely, ridiculously cold!

Hamza Khan (10)

Our Lady Of Mount Carmel Catholic Primary School, Ashton-Under-Lyne

The Colourful Dolphin

There once was a dolphin called Lilly,
Sometimes she acted very silly.
She lived in the sea
Where she was free.
She changes colour
Just like her mother.

Abigail Mayers (10)

Our Lady Of Mount Carmel Catholic Primary School, Ashton-Under-Lyne

Overcome The Obstacle

Listen to me carefully
And a lot you shall learn,
Listen to me carefully
And a lot you shall earn.

Loving, learning, caring,
Don't forget the sharing.
Listen to this poem
And you're heading the right way.
Listen to this poem
And you'll enjoy your day.

Laughing, learning, having fun,
There's always room for improvement on this
journey you shall run,
Everybody has a goal,
But they've got to play the role.

Listen to me now
And you'll aim for the skies.
Listen to me now
And you're bound to never have to tell lies.

Your journey never ends,
You'll always find yourself.
Listen very cautiously
And you will find the truth.
Listen very thoughtfully
And you will have an exciting youth.

We've all failed, at something I bet,
But let's call it 'success-not-yet'.
Read this poem carefully
And I hope you quite enjoyed it.
All I can say to you is
Never doubt or worry about,
Take a step and make your shout!

Katie Mann (9)

Queen's Drive Primary School, Fulwood

C.U.P.P.A

One: Do not dare to compare,
Or you will find life very unfair.
People will laugh and not even care.
So for goodness sake,
Get fear out of your hair!

Two: Be very kind,
You never know what others think in their mind.
Keep the past behind!
You had a successful life,
What else did you find?

Three: Be very unique.
Have the guts to go up and speak!
Unique means be different in a good way,
We're all unique!
Be unique and you'll have a good day!

Four: So you got something incorrect?
Just call it success-not-yet.
Life is like a positivity net,
You think you can be positive for a week?
Let's call it a bet!

Five: Do not shed a tear,
It's only one fear!
Bring the right gear,
Put on a smile.
If you do these then people will cheer.

Six: We are out of time,
I guess I shall end this rhyme!

Sarah Leanne Buckler (9)

Queen's Drive Primary School, Fulwood

A Day In Ancient Greece

There was a lot of things to know
About ancient Greece,
One thing I can tell you
Is that there wasn't much peace!

The country is busy,
Full of people who were unfair,
They wouldn't give their slaves money,
As this action was very rare.

Their beliefs were a bit abnormal
And even a bit strange,
With all the different gods,
Made from skills of a different range.

All the Greeks looked up to Hercules,
The hero who was given more than one quest,
They tried to copy him move by move,
Because he thought he was the best.

Another thing to know,
Is about Eurystheus who was a king,

He was weak, cruel and selfish,
He brought unhappiness, cruelty and that sort of
thing.

I am glad I live now,
And not in that unfair time,
I wouldn't have survived,
Because I think the Greeks went across the line.

Amirah Vorajee (9)

Queen's Drive Primary School, Fulwood

Power Of Greek Gods!

Zeus is great, god of skies,
As he is also very wise.
He threw lots of vicious bolts,
When it is surely not his fault.
He is our respectful god, Zeus,
Who has never been abused.
Zeus is god of all kings,
Who always does good things.

Poseidon is god of the oceans,
Who never goes in slow motion.
He makes lots of deadly floods,
All across the deadly woods,
He makes lots of scary waves,
That nobody can be saved.
Poseidon is really powerful and strong,
Always believe me or you'll be wrong.

Hades is a god of the Underworld,
While Zeus is in the Thunderworld.
Hades take the people, who are dead,

Onto the giant, fierce, hot bed,
Hades is very mighty and cruel,
Where people think he's quite a fool.
He always gets evil and bad,
When he turns crazy and mad.

Avneesh Desai (9)

Queen's Drive Primary School, Fulwood

Fear Is Near!

It was as if I was being zapped in the back with
fear.
Then suddenly I heard a flap.

The wing of a bird
Or the head of a bat,
the tail of a monkey
Or the fin of a fish.

Why pick on me, Fear?
What have I done?
Fear, oh Fear, leave me alone.
Fear, oh Fear, what have I done?

I heard a thump
In my heart,
Or was it a beat on my toe?
A flabbergasted achoo!

Oh gosh, oh gosh,
I don't know what to do!

Fear is near...
Fear is almost completely clear.

Is it my end?
I can smell it from here...

Fear is here
And it feels like a spear.
Fear is here
And I want it to disappear.
Fear is here
And I am going to cry a tear.
Fear is here
And I don't want this to happen next year.

Isabel Cole (9)

Queen's Drive Primary School, Fulwood

Gods Of Greece

Artemis is god of the moon,
But don't worry, there's another god soon,
Her twin brother,
They came from the same mother,
It's Apollo, he is god of the sun,
Although he likes his daily bread bun,
Ares was god of war and boy he can run,
Although I doubt he was really fun,
Time for more power,
Poseidon was no weak flower,
He was god of the ocean blue
And very intelligent too,
Zeus was the almighty king,
He was married to Hera; don't need no diamond
ring.
Hades was god of the Underworld,
Where all the spirits and souls whirled,
Chronos had a scheming plot,
To eat his children, all the lot,
Hermes was the messenger god,
He had winged sandals; no need to plod,

Hercules had killed a lion, one you can't stroke,
He ripped its skin and wore it like a cloak.

Sujit Reddy Velagala (9)

Queen's Drive Primary School, Fulwood

Be Yourself

Don't dare to compare
Because it's not fair.

Always be yourself, always be unique
It doesn't matter if people call you a freak.

Always be you
Don't be silly, you don't need a crew.

Being caring
Isn't daring.

Always be you
That's all you have to do.

Always be kind
It will happen to you, you'll find.

We all have failed I bet
But let's call it success - not yet!

Don't ever worry
When you improve, no need to hurry.

Happiness is something we all need to show
So don't ever act like you don't know.

You don't need everything to go your way
Just carry on and have a great day.

Lily Beatrice Cornall (9)
Queen's Drive Primary School, Fulwood

Greek Gods

Long ago in ancient Greece
Where myths were told of Jason and the Golden
Fleece,
The land was full of peace
Zeus and his thunderbolt,
Which was sent without a fault,
Suddenly there's a flash,
If I was there I'd make a dash.

Hercules, that awesome hero,
He's better than Emperor Nero.
He's extremely strong,
But his sweat must pong
As the Greeks ate fish
Which was a main dish.

Many men went off to war,
Still, they were not sure,
Hoping for the god of war, to help.
Shame Ares was a coward so the men would just
yelp.
Do your teachers call you mysterious?

I'll tell you a god who is extremely devious.
He shoots arrows, not my idea of love.

Hudhaifah Kazi (9)
Queen's Drive Primary School, Fulwood

What Is Confidence?

What is confidence?
I hear people say,
Confidence is something which helps you on your
way.

Being unique is the key,
After the poem,
You will see!

What is confidence?
I hear them say,
It is something in the mind which will stay.

Positivity is what you need,
I'm sure you can do it,
You and me.

What is confidence?
Well now you know.

Do your best, and off you go!

Amnah Patel (9)
Queen's Drive Primary School, Fulwood

96

Myths And Legends

M any have tried and failed,
Y oung and old have sailed,
T o where vicious beasts attack weak prey,
H ow they got there? A boat or ship will do,
S o great battles are held at their arrival.

A fter a fight, they might become legends,
N ew ones are usually noticed quickly,
D on't fret, well, not yet.

L ost over time,
E veryone learns the very lines,
G one and learnt it at school,
E veryone thought it was cool,
N o one thought about travelling back in time,
D id they or did they not?
S omeone should invent a time machine for
   everyone to see what happened.

Asha Grace Al Alawi (9)
Queen's Drive Primary School, Fulwood

The Three Brothers Of Mischief

Down in Greece people brag,
About their o' so wonderful flag.
They could go on all day
And go on all night,
But what really should give you a fright,
Is the gods who were not frauds.

First came Zeus with his thunder,
Which made me wonder!
How powerful could he be?
Surely not as strong as Poseidon, god of the sea
With his ocean great,
He was Zeus' best mate.
Then came Hades in Hell,
He was in Hell because, well...
He was bad,
But now Cerberus drives him mad,
But he's still a cool god,
To kill you, he only has to nod!

So remember never mess with the gods
And don't call them frauds.

Dillon Bennison (9)
Queen's Drive Primary School, Fulwood

Jason And The Greeks

The ancient Greeks
Fished in blue creeks.
They ate chubby, squawking geese,
Reading 'Jason and the Golden Fleece'.

Jason sailed to war,
Even though he was not sure.
He travelled at age forty-four.

He was very hot
But never lost a shot
Because that was not his plot.

He became King of Greece,
Sometimes wore the golden fleece,
That's because he wanted peace.

He never forgot
About his special pot
Because to him it meant a lot.

Everyone thought of him
Because he was as strong as tin.
So everyone wanted him to be the best king.

Mohammed Deen Saleh (9)

Queen's Drive Primary School, Fulwood

The Trio Of Gods

Long ago in ancient Greece,
While reading Jason and the Golden Fleece,
Artemis was the the god of the moon,
But there was another god coming soon,
Apollo was the god of the sun,
Even though he likes making his hand-made bread
bun.

It's very hot,
Let's make a daily made Greek pot,
Why not?
Zeus was the god of thunder and storms,
Although he does like his ready-made corns.
Zeus has a lightning bolt,
But he is not scared to make it your fault.
As time flashed,
The lightning bolt bashed.

Now you know all the information about
The three gods go and visit them.

Saarah Patel (9)

Queen's Drive Primary School, Fulwood

Spooky Halloween

On a dark, dark night,
you can get a fright.
So please be aware,
Or you'll be in for a scare.

On the 31st October,
You might get a tap on the shoulder,
Because then it will be Halloween
And everyone will turn green.

When the sky turns to a different shade of dark
And you can hear the dog bark
Don't forget to say a prayer
For God to keep you in His care.

Stay clear of all the ghosts and monsters
Because at times they can drive you bonkers,
The time has come because it's Halloween night,
Remember to stay clear of the ghost in white.

Scott Bradley (9)
Queen's Drive Primary School, Fulwood

Ancient Greek Food

One day there was a man who loved to cook.
He cooked in a pot,
But he didn't use a book.
He made the food hot.

He served in a bowl,
He made fish a lot,
For the people in the hall.

Nothing was wasted,
Not even meat,
Because everything was tasted
Even wheat.

People came to the hall every day
To eat his delicious food.
Most of them ate fish from the bay,
All the food was chewed.

Soon he got rich with money
So he bought the whole hall
And started to sell honey,
Then he bought an expensive bowl.

Hashim Ahmed Kazi (9)
Queen's Drive Primary School, Fulwood

Gory Greeks

The Greeks are famous for their gore,
They love it so much they want more and more.
They don't care if they commit murders,
They just want lots of myrrh.

They rip and tear flesh,
They give people the look of mesh.
Their fists are cannonballs,
They are the reason for many falls.

Arrows and spears
Shoot past my ears.
Blood-curdling cries,
My friend dies.

The clip-clop of horses,
They support the armed forces.
Cruel is their ruler,
His followers think he couldn't be cooler.

Srainya Arakal (9)
Queen's Drive Primary School, Fulwood

Spooks

On a horrific night,
I had a terrible fright,
I tried to stay strong like a knight,
I used all my might.

I saw a chubby ghost,
I wondered if it was me who was going to roast!

I ran as fast as my legs could go,
But the ghost was a little too slow.

The Halloween scene?
I'm not so keen.
I heard a creak,
I didn't make a squeak,
Although it was just a leak.

Roars and screams,
I hope this is just a dream,
The monster looks like whipped cream.

Maisie-Belle Molloy (9)
Queen's Drive Primary School, Fulwood

Halloween

Halloween is so good,
Let's all head to the wood.

We went for a run,
It was so fun.

A very funny scene,
Not very clean.

Lots of sweets,
Too many beats.

Let's go for a treat,
Down from the street.

Now for a dare,
I'll take a glare.

That's not fair,
I just can't bear.

What's that over there
Down by the square?

I want a pumpkin,
Let's go jumpin'.

Hibbah Maryam Patel (9)
Queen's Drive Primary School, Fulwood

Untitled

There were the ancient Greeks,
They were dying for the golden fleece.
They all were going to have a battle,
They heard a little noise like a rattle.
There was very heavy rain,
Many people were in pain.

Many people didn't dare,
To fight or even share.
The battle was never going to end,
Their swords were about to bend.

They were gone a long time ago,
How do you know?
Zeus can throw thunderbolts with all his might,
All his thunderbolts are very bright.

Aafiyah Patel (9)
Queen's Drive Primary School, Fulwood

A Heart Of Confidence

Do you know how to succeed,
Being confident in life?
Well, just believe and achieve,
Still worried, use this advice.

One, be really kind,
Then you will see that
You will easily find
Friends everywhere you go!

Secondly, never dare to compare,
Just be unique
And you should care and share,
Be the best version of you.

Never give in,
Create a heart of positivity,
Put your worries in a bin.
We all have different qualities.

Arya Jayakrishnan (9)
Queen's Drive Primary School, Fulwood

The Old Greek Man Who Loved To Cook

One day there was an old Greek man who loved to cook
But he didn't use a book.
His food was hot
So he used a titanium pot.
He also cooked fish and meat a lot.

He cooked some meat, but using no wheat.
He ate lots of geese,
While reading 'Jason and the Golden Fleece'.

The old man cooked in a hall
Where all there was was the shape of a ball.
Then he gained lots of money,
So he started to sell honey
And that's the last line of all.

Ibrahim Moosa (9)
Queen's Drive Primary School, Fulwood

Confidence

Don't have doubt and always be unique,
If you be unique, you'll reach your peak.
Believe in yourself and always be resilient,
Never stop believing and you'll be brilliant.

Why be mean when you can be keen?
When you're keen you'll have a great team.
We all have failure inside I bet,
But let's just call it, 'success not yet'.

Always try hard and be the best version of you,
Don't be sad and have a 'can do' attitude.

Anand Singh (10)
Queen's Drive Primary School, Fulwood

A Spooky Tale

The spook comes at night,
Giving you a fright,
Every day and night,
Oh my! Oh my!
Giving me a bite.

As dark as a black knight,
Standing in the shadow light,
Out of sight,
Peeking out the building site,
Coming back in sight,
Killing my mice night by night.

What do I do?
Where do I go?
Where is my home?
I just want to be safe
Where the normal world is off my case.
Just let me tie my shoelace.

Adam Member (9) & Aimee Jade Tilley
Queen's Drive Primary School, Fulwood

Ancient Greece

Down in Greece people brag,
Brag about their wonderful flag,
But that is not all; the children brag too,
Not about their flag,
No, not about their flag, but about winning tag,
It made the other children very sad.

The gods talked to the goddesses
And often one confesses,
About Poseidon cheating on Amphitrite,
For a human!

Lightning means Zeus is furious,
Which makes people curious,
To know what has made him angry.

Megan Casey (10)
Queen's Drive Primary School, Fulwood

Cuppa's Fantastic Journey

Cuppa is fair,
He doesn't want to compare.
He doesn't want to share
And he wants to care.

He is fabulous, but never miraculous,
He knows how to keep the flow
But he doesn't know how to row.

Cuppa is known as unique
And can never become a freak.
Cuppa can be cool,
But is such a fool.

The Mac twins are rude
And are total noobs,
Jack Mac is mean
And when fighting he is very keen.

Eesaa Member (9)
Queen's Drive Primary School, Fulwood

Hercules The Hero

Have you ever heard of ancient Greece,
I'm going to give you a lovely treat.

We are going to talk about Hercules,
The hero that went to Café Nero,
The star that went far in his car.

He faced scary monsters,
Some were hairy,
Some were even called Mary.

He strangled them from an angle,
While dangling from a candle.

He stood at the top of the stairs,
While he plucked their hair.

Poppy Billington (9)
Queen's Drive Primary School, Fulwood

Untitled

On a deadly night
I was filled with fright.
I tried to be brave
With all my might
But I failed and cried.

Suddenly I saw a ghost
And it was pretty weird,
'Cause me it was gonna roast.
Am I its Halloween dinner
Or am I just gonna be toast?

The question is was it good or bad
Or was it just really mad?
Who doesn't know and who does?
Well, I'm gonna buzz
Because this is really tough.

Medhansh Nandwana (9)
Queen's Drive Primary School, Fulwood

The Mouse In The House

In the house
There was a mouse
That ate a plate
That was going out of date,
Until a bright light appeared
But the mouse showed his might
And walked to the ghost
While eating some toast,
The mouse stared like he didn't care
In the face of the ghost,
The mouse was scared
And then said, 'Want to share?'
The ghost stood still until the moon came out,
When he picked up the spoon
And decided to dig in and divide.

Blake Hallas (10)
Queen's Drive Primary School, Fulwood

Greek Gods

G reek gods were always bold

R ather a lot of tales have been told

E ven though Hermes is as fast as a bolt

E lsewhere Eros can make you fall in love but it's not your fault

K ing of the gods, almighty Zeus.

G oddess Hera won't call a truce

O n Mount Olympus haven't you heard?

D o sacrifices and the gods will keep their word

S ee Zeus with his thundering rod!

Omar Abdou (9)

Queen's Drive Primary School, Fulwood

The Haunted House

Deep in the dark house,
I was searching around
And then I heard a mouse.

There was something that gave me a fright,
I looked around
And it was only a light.

Where was the light coming from?
I thought,
Oh, I was missing my mum.

I was so scared
And then I saw something,
Something that was long-haired.

Oh no, I better run,
Off I go,
What have I done?

Eva Dawson (9)
Queen's Drive Primary School, Fulwood

Recipe For Being Unique

First of all if you want to be unique
Add in a drop of kindness
And self-esteem to make you confident and brave.
After you would have to sprinkle
A bit of sugar to sweeten sweets up a bit.

Don't copy other people,
Don't be a sheep.
Be the best version of you.
Be as tall as a tree,
Be confident like me.
Don't let the rain pitter-patter,
Make you fail.
Stay away from that failure.

Chloe Donnelly (9)
Queen's Drive Primary School, Fulwood

The Spook Is Back

The spook is out at night
And it's giving me a fright.
The spook is where?
It's under there.

He strangles at lots of angles so beware.
He stands in light with a big dog bite.
The man has scars from a bar where he sat
At the back with a smack.

Now he's dead in his bed,
Oh no he's back from the dead.
Where is he? He's in the bed.
Uh oh! I'm dead...

Thomas Hutton (9)
Queen's Drive Primary School, Fulwood

The Spook's Night!

On a dark night the moon was bright,
The scratching noises were ruining my night!
Loud and clear he cackled, never fear,
Laughing in horror he disappeared.
On a deadly night my life was a fright.
Trick or treat, I want some sweets!
I'm hungry for some meat.
Look out for 31st, the spooks might
Be there in an hour.
Beware, beware he's waiting there
At the door in an hour!
Mwhahahaha...

Aamena Patel (9)
Queen's Drive Primary School, Fulwood

Untitled

The Greek god, Zeus
Got sacrifices
Often a goose
He shot thunder
Which made me wonder
He created lightning
Which was frightening.

He made the ocean
With a lot of commotion
He is very fast
Which made me gasp
Ares is strong
And Eros is wrong.

Zeus is god of the sky
And I don't know why
He heard a roar
That sounded like a boar or even a Minotaur.

Jaxon (9)
Queen's Drive Primary School, Fulwood

Greek Gods Rule

Zeus is the king of gods,
After a lot of work he will not stop.

When Aries turns pale,
It means he has failed.
He goes on quests,
So he is the best.

Hades was sad,
Because he made everybody mad.
'What have I done?' he wailed.
He remembered he set an attack
And got caught by his mother!
What a bother!

Greek gods are so cool,
Greek gods rule!

Aidan Lee (9)
Queen's Drive Primary School, Fulwood

I Can't Get To Sleep

Fixed in bed nice and warm
But I can't go to sleep,
Shadows are appearing,
Curtains are waving,
Fear is coming here,
Wolves are howling as night is coming,
My hands are shaking,
The sounds are clear,
I saw the monster in a fright,
I could use a little bit of light,
It was really dark, I could hear Rex bark,
Oh no, who's that?
Help, help, is someone really near...?

Mariyah Musa (9)
Queen's Drive Primary School, Fulwood

Speak Out Loud

If you work in a team
It will help achieve your dreams.
Whenever you feel sad
Just think about happy thoughts and everything
will be fab.

Confidence we all show
Whenever we need it the most.
Speak out loud
Then you will find happiness around.

Challenges are sometimes very hard to do
But sometimes they are good for you,
Be unique and show your technique.

Lucie Smith (9)
Queen's Drive Primary School, Fulwood

Greece's Most Beautiful Beaches

Out in the sun which is burning hot,
You're running to the sea collecting water in your pot,
This is Greece,
You don't need to wear coats made of fleece,
Relax in peace,
Open up your backback,
On your back will lay ice packs,
Build a castle made with sand,
Of course made with your hands,
I won't tell,
You were out in the back,
Ready to go hiding your rucksack.

Amber Hussain (9)
Queen's Drive Primary School, Fulwood

Horror's Here

Doom is here,
The moon is near,
Wings flap,
Creatures crawl,
Deer is coming with fear,
Horror's here.

The signs are clear,
Horror's here
With unluckiness,
It is all near,
Fears all clear.

It is coming together now,
Horror's here,
Is it the end?
It is crystal-clear,
Far and near,
October is here.

Zara Mann (9)
Queen's Drive Primary School, Fulwood

Ancient Greeks

Have you ever heard of ancient Greeks?
Well I'm going to give you a sneaky peak.

Let's start off with the mighty gods,
Who really liked to eat pea pods.

Now let's go on to Hercules,
The hero who had mighty fleas.

War! War! War!
When it came to war
The Greeks were poor.
What a typical war
It was in Greece.

Anoosha Khan (10)
Queen's Drive Primary School, Fulwood

Horror Halloween!

One dark night I had a fright,
It was a pitch-black night.
Beware on the 31st of October,
As there might be a shudder.
So look out for the full moon
As it might come too soon.
Make sure you don't go to Death's door,
As rich and poor are at the front door.
Do not glance at the deadly ghost,
As there might be a last chance.

Amirah Patel (9)

Queen's Drive Primary School, Fulwood

Oh No, Halloween!

On a winter's night
I got quite a fright,
As the moon shone
It started to get bright.

I was struck with fear,
It all looked clear,
This was the year
Halloween was near.

There I stood,
In my fluffy white hood,
It didn't look good.

Beware,
It sat there,
In its little lair.

Amirah Adnan Ahmed (9)
Queen's Drive Primary School, Fulwood

Everybody Is Unique

Everybody is unique
With their voice they can speak.
You can hear positive thoughts
You will succeed at being a good sport.

Confidence is what you need
Self-belief will help you succeed,
Always be kind
Then you will feel happiness inside.

But everybody is unique
So don't think you are a freak!

Ebony Julianne Cerqua (10)
Queen's Drive Primary School, Fulwood

The Big Scare

On a spooky night
I froze with fright,
I was feeling brave
So I went within the dark cave!

I won't be ready for a scare,
I will be ready to tear,
But I don't dare
To do a big jump scare!

I think I saw a ghost,
Or was it me making toast?
I think I saw a beast,
Or was it a high priest?

Zakaria Ahmed (10)
Queen's Drive Primary School, Fulwood

Fear Is Here

Fear is here,
As the creepy-crawlies come near,
It's crystal-clear,
Fear is here.

Demons reappear,
Towards me ghosts career,
Every single year.
It is just so clear,
Fear is here.

Far and near,
Fear is here.

It's all coming together,
October is near!

Anna Bradford (9)
Queen's Drive Primary School, Fulwood

The Confident Mind

The confident mind,
Not everyone likes their positivity,
But if you take the opportunity,
Then you can enjoy any fun activity.
Do you know that you are unique
And always try to make your confidence reach the peak.
With your own voice you will always speak!
Do not dare to compare
Because it's just not fair.

Muhammad Randeri (9)
Queen's Drive Primary School, Fulwood

Night

At night you'll get a scare,
Over there to be fair.
You will die like a fly,
Not a lie, don't know why.

You are no match for a catch.
The cat is no hat nor a monster.
Go! Go faster!
Till the end such stretch.

What the heck
For the neck.

Andrew Richard Hugh Donaldson (9)
Queen's Drive Primary School, Fulwood

The Return Of The Spook

The spook is out at night
And giving me a fright,
Every day and every night
Giving me a bite.
In the shadow in my time of bed at night,
Out of the light.

Oh my, oh my,
Giving a holey black bite out of the night,
Standing in the shadow of the light.

Ibraheem Aziz (9)
Queen's Drive Primary School, Fulwood

In The Future

In the future I think I'll be
A submarine driver under the sea,
Up, up, up we swoosh. 1... 2... 3... *Whoosh!*
In the future I think I'll be a plane driver,
High swooping through the air,
I go back down with a big, big glare,
In the future I think I'll be a car driver
Clutching down on the accelerator with the wheels
Spinning and turning.
Feels like they're really burning,
In the future I think I'll be a firefighter,
Saving a cat in a tree.
This is what I want to be,
So don't be afraid to tell me
What do you want to be?

Daisy Gittins (7)
St Agnes CE Primary School, Lees

My Favourite Band

My favourite rock band is called Queen,
They are the best rock band you could have seen.
Their music is loud, I feel very proud,
When Freddie, Brian, John and Roger go on stage,
They sound like an old man full of rage.
Freddie was the best singer
And songwriter there has ever been.
When I hear 'I Want To Break Free',
I get goosebumps all around me.
Queen's music makes me happy,
It makes me sing and dance whenever I get the chance.
Their music will be with me,
It's a shame tickets to see them are not free!

Logan Allison (8)
St Agnes CE Primary School, Lees

Moving House

Photos taken, house for sale,
Arranging viewings by email.
Viewers arriving, showing them round,
Upstairs, downstairs worth every pound.

House is sold, a new story to be told,
Packing up toys, games and even my clothes.
Not long now till we're on our way,
I'm so excited for moving in day.

The day we've been waiting for, our new family fort
And meeting new friends here in our court.
I like my new bedroom, carpet so soft,
Plenty of space to play and even a loft.

Joshua White (9)
St Agnes CE Primary School, Lees

Slow Beau

In a little town called Oldham
There is a little nook called Daisy
Where lives the pony prince, Beau
But I call him Slow Beau.

He is black and brown
And never frowns,
and can be a little naughty,
But I love Slow Beau.

We walk, trot and canter
And have a little banter,
That's what I love about little Prince Beau.

Isabella Josephine Holcroft (7)
St Agnes CE Primary School, Lees

I Dream A Dream

Every night I go to bed,
I dream of fairies in my head.
I grow my wings that sparkle and shine
So I can fly up high into the night.
There is a magic inside me where anything is
possible.
Fairyland, I don't want to leave
But the sun's coming up so my dream must end,
But I'll be back tonight to see you again.

Scarlett Summer Lees (8)

St Agnes CE Primary School, Lees

Dangerous Mobs

The night is a fright
Because of creepers' delight.
You would want to stay out of their sight.
Endermen steal blocks,
Zombies moan and bang.
Ghosts moan when they're in a moaning zone.
Ender Dragons prey for someone to slay,
So to all the mobs out there
Because Steve won't play for another day.

Ethan Smith (10)
St Agnes CE Primary School, Lees

Jurassic World

Dinosaurs stomp all around,
Making footprints in the ground.
Swishing their long tails,
Everywhere you go you can hear their loud wails.
Scratching with their diamond-like claws,
Crunching bones with their huge jaws.
Feet like motorbikes running fast everywhere,
While pteranodons fly high in the air.

William Thomas Sever (7)
St Agnes CE Primary School, Lees

Pets

Cats that purr, dogs that woof,
Bunny rabbits' tails like white fluff.
Spooky spiders and minibeasts,
Snakes that hiss and enjoy a feast.
Bearded lizards and furry mice
But none of them like rice.
These are pets but if you love them
Just don't forget to tell them so.

Emily Grace Bertram (7)

St Agnes CE Primary School, Lees

Lola The English Bull Terrier

Lola big and strong,
Brown and white,
Very lazy, always sleeping.
Hungry every minute of the day!
Sniffing around me when I have my tea,
Stubborn when out walking and won't come home.
Licks my feet when I am sat on the sofa.
I love my cuddly snuggly Lola.

Ava Grace McNally (8)
St Agnes CE Primary School, Lees

Minecraft

M ultiple mini games to play.

I rresistible bosses like the Ender Dragon or the Wither.

N ever go to the Nether, something fatal might happen!

E asy, normal or hard mode to play.

C reepers come out at night.

R edstone contraptions to turn your lights on.

A nimals to breed with seeds and wheat.

F ight all those skeletons and get yourself a bow.

T ry to finish the game, you'll notice you can't.

Oliver Tucker (9)

St Bartholomew's CE Primary School, Great Harwood

When I Grow Up

When I grow up will I have friends?
Will the grass even be green?

Will humans walk?
Will fish swim?

When I grow up will humans talk?
Will tigers roar?

Will everything be black, white or even grey?
Will cheerleaders cheer?
Will runners run?
Will rocks wriggle?
Will worms stay still?

What will happen when I grow up?
I don't know.

Jessica Catherine Rowe (8)
St Bartholomew's CE Primary School, Great Harwood

The Riddle

Go to the clock behind,
It may be a surprise,
Then read it,
Then it might give a clue.

Bang the top right wall
And it might be another surprise.
The surprise might be $10,000 note.
Go left or right,
But remember right isn't always right.

Connor Lewis Woods (8)
St Bartholomew's CE Primary School, Great Harwood

My Beautiful Daisy

Daisy, daisy, please come out!
Your petals are so white,
Like white tentacles upon your back.
Your stalk is so green
Like a shivering leaf upon your skin.
Your flower is so beautiful,
As beautiful as a shiny yellow hat.

Tara McIntosh (9)

St Bartholomew's CE Primary School, Great Harwood

Summer

S un, sea and sand
U nforgettable holidays
M arvellous days out
M aking memories with family and friends
E ating out somewhere nice
R elaxing in the sun eating ice cream.

Katie Balderson (10)

St Bartholomew's CE Primary School, Great Harwood

School Daze

(A kennings poem)

Fidget spinner
Bottle flipper
Teacher pleaser
Desk sitter
Friend maker
Friend breaker
Smile giver
Homework hater
Dinner eater
Football player
Job doer
Daydreamer.

Joshua Duckworth (9)

St Bartholomew's CE Primary School, Great Harwood

Summer Fun

It's summer! Hooray! It's summer today.
Let's go outside and turn the music on.
On the swings, in the pool, let's jump in, hooray!
Let's get the bouncy ball and play.
Oh no! It's gone!

Time for the beach today, let's play.
It's fun on the beach, we get to build things.
Let's get some ice cream, it's really fun, yay!
Look, there's a butterfly, look at it,
especially its wings.

The sun is so hot like a fire flaming!
It's really fun here, it's the best here.
This is really fun, it's better than video gaming,
Oh look! Rides and a café on the pier.

It's time to go, hopefully we will come back
next time,
Look at the coloured beach ball, it looks like mine.

Chloe Chaffer (9)
St John With St Michael CE Primary School, Shawforth

Under Tale Story

You're called Frisk, you fell in a big hole,
You were greeted by flowers but evil flowers.
Once you fell down a flower tricks you to steal your soul.
For some odd reason it smells a little sour.

It's Toriel, yay Toriel!
She takes you to her yellow home.
Her chair's called Chariel.
You leave because you want to eat your own food at home.

You go to Snowdin Town,
It's very snowy and white.
You meet Sans who never wears a frown,
then you see Papyrus, he has a red cape
And he is brighter.

Then after waterfall to Hot Land,
Then to Asgare's castle.
I try so hard to finish Asgare's battle.

Charlie Careswell (8)
St John With St Michael CE Primary School, Shawforth

Cheery Merry Christmas

I am having a delightful Christmas tea,
Christmas has come!
I am putting up my Christmas tree,
My dad says, 'Yippee! Christmas has come!'

It's almost Christmas Day, let's go to bed!
Oh my gosh, it's almost Christmas Day.
'It's almost Christmas Day,' I said,
I went to my friend's house to stay.

All night long we played,
When I got home I saw the Christmas tree.
I bought a sledge,
For tea I had it for free.

Shh! Don't forget to not wake Santa
For my present I got a manta.

Cameron Rae Blackburn-Smith (7)

St John With St Michael CE Primary School, Shawforth

Maisie

Marching Maisie is so cute.
Marching Maisie is so mad.
Marching Maisie chews my boots.
Marching Maisie is so glad.

Mad Maisie is so warm.
Mad Maisie is so smooth.
Mad Maisie is scared of storms.
Mad Maisie knows a lot of moves.

Moody Maisie is so moody.
Moody Maisie sleeps all day.
Moody Maisie loves a lot of food.
Moody Maisie hates the colour grey.

Caitlin Taylor (7)
St John With St Michael CE Primary School, Shawforth

Shining Summer

Summer is fun!
Summer is hot,
Summer is still fun in the sun
Like a huge boiling pot.

Summer is a happy place.
Summer holidays come too soon!
But it could burn your face!
When the bells ring we all go through the door,
We all go boom!

Summer is cool,
Summer is fun,
Even when you're in a cold swimming pool,
Especially in the sun.

Summer is fun,
Not just in the sun.

Natalie Varnom (7)
St John With St Michael CE Primary School, Shawforth

My Little Cute Dog

My little puppy is so fluffy,
He has a tiny nose.
He gets cuter every time he grows.
He has such cute eyes,
He sounds loud every time he cries.
He can jump so high,
It's like he's flying through the sky.
My dog is really jumpy,
Sometimes he is really grumpy.

Bailey Fletcher (8)

St John With St Michael CE Primary School, Shawforth

Winter

W e like snow, it comes from the sky

  I nside we have hot chocolate

N ice and warm when we go inside

  T asty hot chocolate

  E arly morning to open the presents on Christmas

  R ead a new book from Christmas Day.

Imogen Steel (7)

St John With St Michael CE Primary School, Shawforth

School

S chool is the best

C ome to St John with St Michael's

H olly is my best friend

O melette is my favourite dinner at my school

O pen the door, everybody barges in

L ove spreads in our school.

Natasha Holmes (7)

St John With St Michael CE Primary School, Shawforth

Animals

A mazing owls

N ature

I love owls

M onkeys going crazy

A nimals playing in the leaves

L ions in their snuggly beds

S leeping animals.

Libby Duff (9)

St John With St Michael CE Primary School, Shawforth

YOUNG WRITERS INFORMATION

We hope you have enjoyed reading this book – and that you will continue to in the coming years.

If you're a young writer who enjoys reading and creative writing, or the parent of an enthusiastic poet or story writer, do visit our website **www.youngwriters.co.uk**. Here you will find free competitions, workshops and games, as well as recommended reads, a poetry glossary and our blog.

If you would like to order further copies of this book, or any of our other titles, then please give us a call or visit **www.youngwriters.co.uk**.

Young Writers
Remus House
Coltsfoot Drive
Peterborough
PE2 9BF
(01733) 890066
info@youngwriters.co.uk